PUSS IN BOOTS

by
Charles Perrault

Illustrated by
Andrea DaRif

Troll Associates

Troll Associates, Mahwah, N.J.

Library of Congress Catalog Card Number: 78-18061
ISBN 0-89375-130-8

Once there was a poor miller who died and left everything he owned to his three sons. Dividing the belongings was easy, for the miller had only three things: a mill, a donkey, and a cat named Puss. The oldest son got the mill, the middle son took the donkey, and the youngest was left the cat.

"What good is a cat?" grumbled the youngest son.
The cat looked at his new master and said, "Perhaps
I can be more useful than you think. Just get me a sack
and a pair of hunting boots, and you shall see."

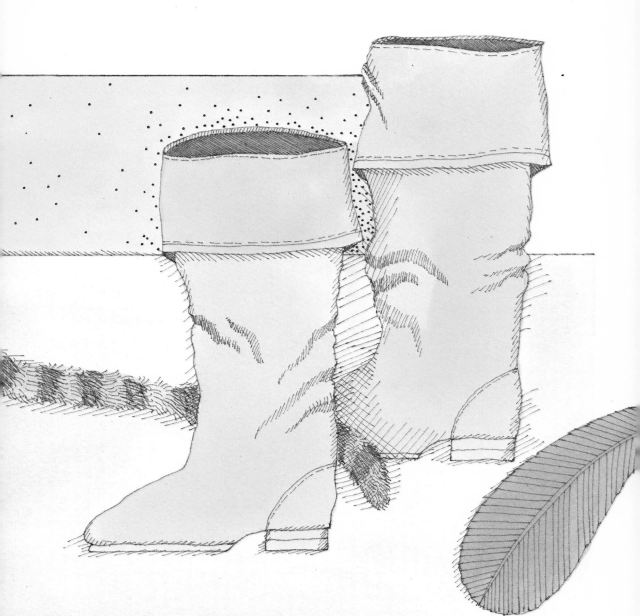

Now the miller's son knew that Puss had shown great skill in catching rats and mice. And surely a cat who could talk must be clever indeed! So he decided to get Puss the sack and the boots.

When Puss got the boots, he pulled them on. Then he threw the sack over his shoulder, and marched off. Soon he came to a place where he knew there were plenty of rabbits. He put some bran and some lettuce into the bag. Before long, a fat, foolish rabbit hopped up and began to eat the lettuce. Puss yanked on the drawstring, and caught the rabbit!

Puss marched far away to a king's palace, with the rabbit in his sack. He bowed before the king and said, "Your majesty, this rabbit is a gift from my master, the Marquis of Carabas."

The king took the rabbit and said, "Tell your master that I gladly accept his thoughtful gift."

Several days later, Puss took his sack into a field and caught two partridges. He presented them to the king, saying, "These are from my master, the Marquis of Carabas." Again, the king gladly accepted the gift.

One day, Puss learned that the king was planning to ride through part of the countryside he had never seen before. The king's daughter—the most beautiful princess in the world—would ride with him.

Puss went to his master and said, "If you do exactly as I say, your fortune will soon be made. Go and bathe in the river, and leave the rest to me. But remember, your new name is the Marquis of Carabas."

While the miller's son was bathing in the river, Puss hid his clothes under a rock. Then, when the king's carriage passed the river, Puss cried out, "Help! Help! My master, the Marquis of Carabas, is drowning!"

The king recognized Puss. He stopped the carriage, and sent his guards to save the "drowning" man. Puss told the king that thieves had stolen his master's clothes. "That is no problem," replied the king, and he sent at once for some elegant clothes.

When the miller's son was dressed in the new clothes, he looked exactly like a marquis! The king was pleased to meet him, and the princess thought he was quite handsome. So they invited him to join them in the carriage. The cat ran on ahead, pleased that his plan was working so well.

Soon Puss came to some peasants who were mowing hay in a large meadow. "The king is coming!" he shouted. "When he gets here, you must tell him that this land is owned by the Marquis of Carabas. If you do not, you shall be chopped as small as mincemeat!" The peasants were terrified! So when the king rode by and asked who owned the meadow, they immediately answered, "The Marquis of Carabas."

Then the king turned to the miller's son and said, "Your land is rich, Marquis. This meadow has produced a fine crop of hay."

Meanwhile, Puss ran ahead until he came to a wheat field, where workers were harvesting the wheat. "The king is coming!" he shouted. "If you do not tell him that this wheat belongs to the Marquis of Carabas, you will be chopped as small as mincemeat!" This frightened the workers so much that they promised to do exactly as they were told.

Before long, the king's carriage arrived at the wheat field. The king asked the workers who owned all the wheat, and they fearfully replied, "The Marquis of Carabas, your highness." And again the king turned to the miller's son and congratulated him on the richness of his land and harvest.

The king's carriage rolled on through the countryside. The cat ran on ahead, threatening everyone he met ... so they all told the king that everything belonged to the Marquis of Carabas! The king was very impressed.

At length, the cat came to a huge castle. A terrible ogre
lived in the castle—it was he who owned all the land the
king had been riding through. Puss walked right up to the
door and said, "I could not pass the castle of such a fine
gentleman without stopping to pay my respects." Now
the ogre knew a compliment when he heard one. So he
welcomed the cat, and was just as polite as an ogre can
be.

Then Puss said, "I understand that you have great magical powers. In fact, I have heard that you can even turn yourself into any kind of animal!"

"That's right!" roared the ogre. "And I'll prove it to you!" At once, the ogre turned into a ferocious lion. Puss was so frightened that he fled to the top of the castle. When the ogre was himself again, Puss crept back down, still a little afraid.

"That was a good trick," said the cat. "But it's easy for a big fellow like you to turn into something huge. I don't suppose you could turn into something small—like a rat or a mouse. That would be impossible—even for you!"

"Impossible?" roared the ogre. "Just watch!" Then—
poof—he was gone, and a tiny mouse appeared and
scurried across the floor. This was exactly what Puss had
wanted! He pounced on the mouse ... and that was the
end of the ogre!

By now, the king's carriage had drawn near. Puss ran to the gate. "Welcome, your majesty!" he called. "Welcome to the castle of my master, the Marquis of Carabas."

"What!" cried the king in surprise. Then he turned to the miller's son. "Is this castle yours, too? My, my!"

The miller's son smiled, but said nothing. He po-
litely helped the princess down from the carriage, and
they all went into the castle, where the ogre's servants
prepared them a magnificent feast.

After they had eaten, the king bowed to the miller's
son and said, "I would be honored to have you as my
son-in-law."

And so the miller's son married the princess, and
became known to everyone throughout the land as the
Marquis of Carabas. All the riches that had belonged to
the terrible ogre now became the property of the marquis.

As for Puss, he became a member of the court, and
never had to chase after mice again—except for fun!